Carrot Forest

To the Tea Party

Magical Cupcake Bakery

River of Tears

The White Rabbit's House

Blue Caterpillar Place

erland

Alice in Wonderland

Down the Rabbit Hole

WRITTEN BY
Lewis Carroll

ILLUSTRATED BY
Eric Puybaret

ALICE IN WONDERLAND

Down the Rabbit Hole

A MODERN RETELLING BY
Joe Rhatigan &
Charles Nurnberg

ALICE

was sitting by the river having
an oh-so-ordinary afternoon, when
a White Rabbit
ran by.

Not just any old rabbit, but one
with pink eyes, a red jacket,
and a great big pocket watch.

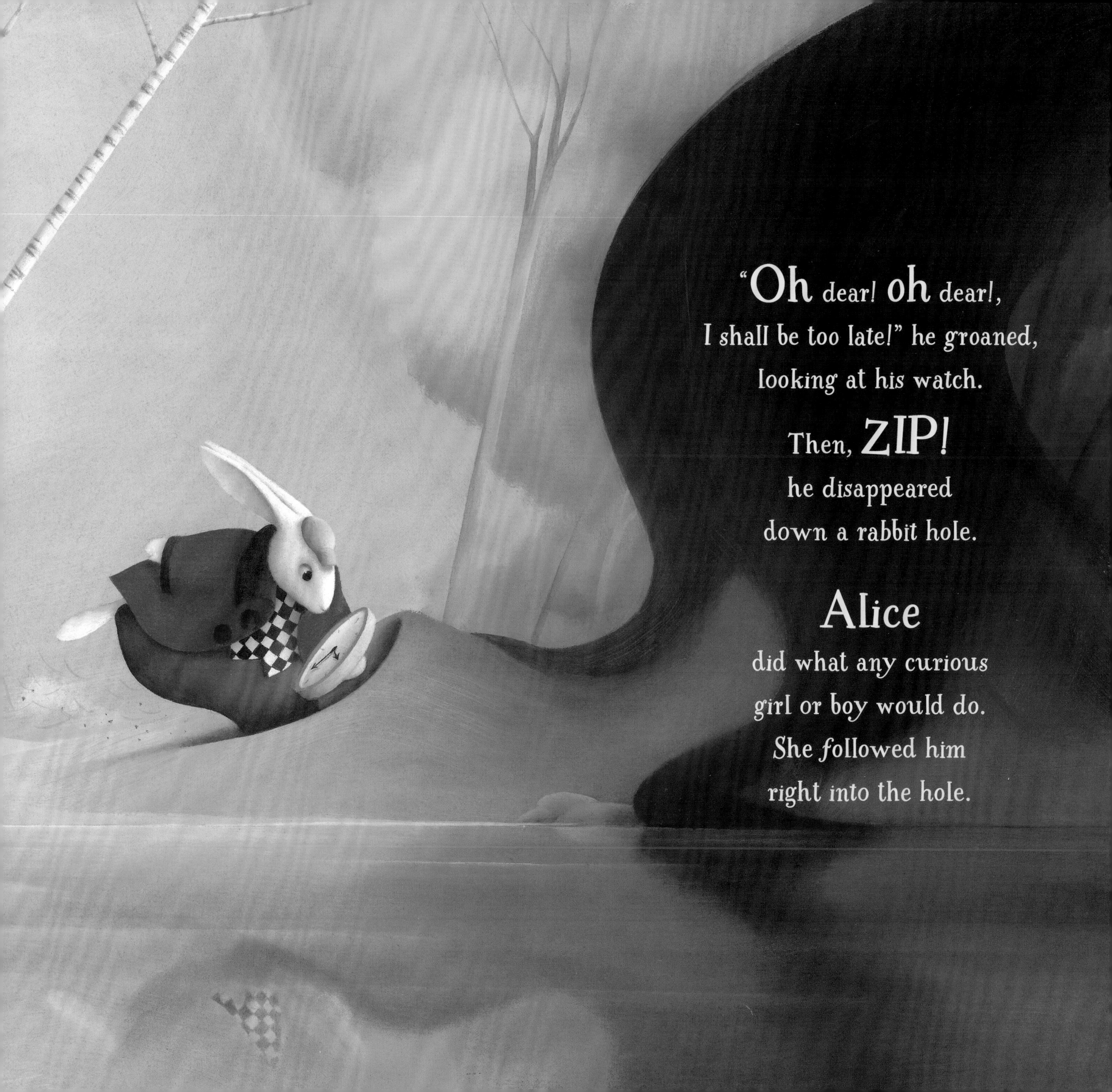

"Oh dear! oh dear!,
I shall be too late!" he groaned,
looking at his watch.

Then, ZIP!
he disappeared
down a rabbit hole.

Alice
did what any curious
girl or boy would do.
She followed him
right into the hole.

DOWN, DOWN, DOWN she fell.

Alice fell for such a long, long time that she thought she might fall all the way through the earth.

Finally, THUMP, THUMP, she landed softly on a pile of leaves and sticks—not hurt at all.

And there was
The White Rabbit,
running down the hallway,
yelling,
"Oh my ears
and whiskers,
how late it's getting!"

The White Rabbit turned
a corner and simply disappeared.
Alice found herself alone in
a long hallway with lots and lots of doors.
On a table was a golden key—a key
that worked on one special, tiny door.

That door opened into the most
beautiful garden Alice had ever seen,
with bright flowers and pretty fountains.
Alice longed to visit the garden.

But she was just too **big** to get through that tiny door.

Perhaps there's a key to
a **bigger** door that will take
me to the garden,
Alice thought.

But instead of another key,
she found a bottle labeled
"DRINK ME."

She thought *for* a minute
and then did exactly that.

"What a curious *feeling*,"
Alice cried,
as she got smaller and smaller.
"I can *fit* through the door now!"

UH OH.

Alice was now so small she couldn't reach the golden key, which she had left on the table.

But under the table Alice found a box with a tiny cake labeled

"EAT ME."

She thought for a minute and then did exactly that.

Suddenly, Alice began to grow

TALLER.

"CURIOUSER AND CURIOUSER!" cried Alice.

"GOODBYE FEET!"

"Now there's no way
I can fit through that tiny door,"
Alice cried.

Buckets of tears fell down
her cheeks, making a big puddle.

ZOOM!

The White Rabbit ran by.
The very **big Alice** scared him,
and he dropped his *fan* and *gloves*
and disappeared.

Alice grabbed the *fan*, which made
her tiny again—so tiny she fell into her river
of tears. She swam and swam,
and soon met up with **Mouse**,
Duck, **Eaglet**, **Dodo**, and a lot of
other interesting animals.

Everyone swam to shore
to dry off by having a race.

Round and round they went until
they were all quite dry.

Alice,

who by now was beginning
to miss her home, said,
"I wish I had my Dinah here.
She's my cat and she's great
at catching mice.
And you should
see her chase the birds."

WOW!

That scary thought
sent all the animals
running off.

WAIT!

What's that sound?

Footsteps?

It was The White Rabbit again!

"Run home this minute and

get my gloves and fan,"

he told Alice.

Alice ran and *found* the house
and the *gloves* and *fan* *inside* . . .
and a *special* bottle, too.

"I know *something* interesting
is bound to happen,"
she said as *she* drank *from* it.

"YIKES! I'm growing."

Alice's head pushed against the ceiling, her *foot* went up the chimney, and an arm stuck out a window.

Frightened by what had happened to Alice, The White Rabbit and his animal friends sent Bill the Lizard down the chimney to see what was going on.

Alice gave him a little kick.

"There goes Bill!"

Alice heard the animals say.

"CATCH HIM!"

The
White Rabbit,
Dodo, Mouse, and all the animals
surrounded the house,
throwing pebbles at
GIANT Alice.

Every stone turned into a small,
magical cake when it hit her.

"I bet I know what will happen if
I eat one,"
Alice said to herself.

Sure enough, after swallowing a cake,
she was soon small enough to
race out the door and escape.

Tiny Alice needed something special to eat to get back to her regular girl size. And then she needed to find her way home.

She saw a giant mushroom with a Blue Caterpillar sitting right on top.

"Eat the mushroom," he said. "One side of it will make you smaller and the other bigger."

One bite and Alice's chin almost hit her feet.

A bite from the other side and her neck grew so LONG her head was soon lost in the clouds.

A few more bites and she finally got to the right size. Phew!